THE
CAT
AND THE
FIDDLER

BY JACKY JETER

PICTURES BY LIONEL KALISH

PARENTS' MAGAZINE PRESS · NEW YORK

TO ISABEL AND
HAROLD GERHARDT,
VERY SPECIAL PARENTS

One morning a fiddler walked through town with his cat
trailing at his heels. Shopkeepers were beginning
to open their shops. Housewives were sweeping their stoops.
The milkman with his cart was just finishing his rounds.

"Pardon me," said the fiddler to the milkman. "I am a stranger in town. Perhaps you could direct me to a place where I might have breakfast."

The milkman smiled and reached down to pat the fiddler's cat.
"Why, of course," he replied. "There is a fine place
just down the street. By the way, this looks
like such a fine cat. Perhaps you would sell her to me."
"Oh, I wouldn't think of selling her," replied the fiddler.
"This is a very special cat."

"I would take good care of her," said the milkman.
"She could catch the mice on my milkcart,
and I would feed her the finest of cream."

"No," smiled the fiddler. "I could not part with her. Watch."
With that he picked up his fiddle,
tucked it under his chin, and began to play a jig.

Suddenly the cat started to dance. First she danced on her
hind paws; then she danced on her front paws.
She whirled around and around, bobbing gracefully
to the tune the fiddler played. Finally, the fiddler stopped.
"As you can see," he said, "she's a very special cat."

By this time, of course, many people had gathered to hear the fiddler play and to watch the cat dance. Now they began to applaud wildly.

"A dancing cat is indeed special," said one of the men.
"Such a fine cat should not be sold just to hunt mice.
Perhaps you would sell her to me.
She could perform in my carnival."

The fiddler shook his head. "Oh, no," he replied.
"I do not intend to sell her at all.
One does not part with such a special cat."
And with that he put his fiddle away
and walked on down the street.

Now the fiddler was in no hurry to leave the town.
He played lullabies for the babies in their carriages.

He played jigs for the children in the park.

He played waltzes for the young people.

He played airs for the old people.
He played something for everyone, and as he did so,
his cat would dance to the music. Everyone loved the cat
and the fiddler; never had the townspeople been so happy.

One day, however, the King heard of the fiddler and his cat. "Send for them at once!" he cried. "I must see what is so special about this pair."

Soon the fiddler and his cat appeared at the palace.
"I want you to amuse me," ordered the King, crossly.
The fiddler bowed low. The cat bowed low.
"It is a privilege to perform for you, your Majesty,"
said the fiddler.

With that he tucked his fiddle under his chin
and began to play. The cat rose on her hind paws
and began to dance. Together they did their best.
Never had the fiddler played so well; never had the cat
danced so splendidly. When they had finished,
the court began to applaud with delight.
"Bravo!" they cried. "Wonderful! Magnificent! Tremendous!"

The King smiled haughtily. "Your performance was indeed well worth my time," he said. "Now what is your price for such a dancing cat?"
"This cat is not for sale, your Majesty," answered the fiddler softly. "This is a very special cat. I could never sell her to anyone because she has no price."
"So it shall be, then," stated the King. "I shall take the cat and give you nothing in return."
Instantly the cat was snatched away from the fiddler.
"Be gone with you," ordered the King.

"But, your Majesty," protested the fiddler,
"don't you wish me to stay and play for you and the cat?"
"What nonsense!" exclaimed the King. "I have musicians
who play one hundred times better than you."
"But this is a very special cat," protested the fiddler.
"I am the only one who—"
It was too late. The poor fiddler was thrown outside.

"Now then," exclaimed the King,
once the fiddler was gone, "let the musicians begin.
I wish to see more of this dancing cat."
The court musicians began to play
and the cat began to dance. One by one,
everyone in the court began to tap their toes.
One by one, the ladies of the court began to dance.
Soon even the King himself was dancing. The cat led
the dance around and around.

Finally, the King grew tired.
"Enough!" he shouted. "The musicians may stop."
But the musicians couldn't stop playing.
"I said enough!" shouted the King. "The ladies and gentlemen may stop dancing."

But the ladies and gentlemen of the court couldn't
stop dancing. Even the King himself couldn't stop dancing.
"Help! Help!" cried the King. "I'm tired.
Cat, stop your dancing. I command you. Stop!"
The cat, however, was not tired. She danced faster
and faster, and everyone else found themselves dancing
faster and faster. The cat danced outside the courtroom.
Everyone followed, dancing.
She danced down the palace steps.
Everyone followed, dancing.

She danced outside the palace gates.
Everyone followed, dancing.
Finally, she danced straight to the fiddler.
"Help us, help us!" gasped the King. "Stop your dancing cat!"
"Ah, but it's not my cat anymore," said the fiddler
with a smile. "Don't you remember, your Majesty?
You took her from me. *You* stop her."
"I can't. I've tried!" cried the King. He could barely
lift his feet, yet he continued to dance.
"I'll give her back to you. Just make her stop dancing!"

The fiddler picked up his fiddle, tucked it under his chin, and began to play softly. Instantly, the King, the ladies and gentlemen of the court, and all the musicians fell exhausted to the ground.

"Come, Puss," said the fiddler to his cat. "We must be on our way." The fiddler continued to play, and the cat continued to dance as they walked down the road.

That night the fiddler patted his cat
while she purred contentedly.
"You are indeed a very special cat," said the fiddler,
"and I shall never part with you."
Then he poured a huge bowl of cream.
Even a very special cat likes cream.

THE END